I0635515

I Can
Read
with
My Eyes Shut!

I Can Read with My Eyes Shut!

By Dr. Seuss

COLLINS

500 665786

Trademark of Random House Inc.
Authorised user HarperCollins*Publishers* Ltd

12   13   14   15   16   17   18   19   20

ISBN 0 00 171331 0 (paperback)
ISBN 0 00 171170 9 (hardback)

© 1978 by Dr. Seuss Enterprises, L.P.
All Rights Reserved
A Beginner Book published by arrangement with
Random House Inc., New York, USA
First published in the UK 1979

Printed and bound in Hong Kong

For

David Worthen, E.G.*

*(Eye Guy)

I can read
in **red.**

I can read
in **blue.**

I can read in
pickle colour
too.

I can read in bed.

And in purple.
And in brown.

I can read
with
my
left eye.

I
can
read
with
my right.

I can read
Mississippi
with my eyes shut tight!

I can read them
with my eyes shut!

That is
VERY HARD
to do!

But it's bad for my hat
and makes my eyebrows
get red hot.
so . . .

reading with my eyes shut
I don't do an awful lot.

And when I keep them open
I can read with much more speed.
You have to be a speedy reader
'cause there's so, so much to read!

You can read about trees . . .

and bees . . .

and knees.

And knees on trees!

And
bees
on
threes!

You can read about anchors.

And all about ants.

You can read
about ankles!

And crocodile pants!

You can read about hoses . . .

and how
to smell roses . . .

and what
you should do
about owls on noses!

Young cat! If you keep
your eyes open enough,
oh, the stuff you will learn!
The most wonderful stuff!

You'll learn about . . .

fishbones . . .   and wishbones.

You'll learn
about trombones,
too.

You'll learn
about Jake
the Pillow Snake

and all about
Foo-Foo the Snoo.

You can learn about ice.

You can learn about mice.

Mice on ice.

And
ice
on
mice.

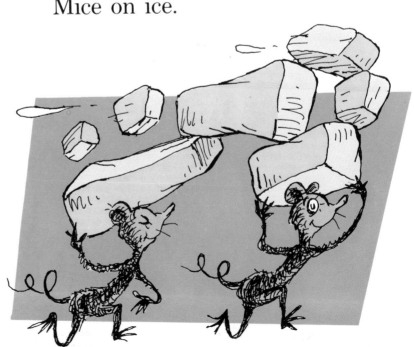

You can learn about
the price of ice.

Nice ice
for sale.
Ten cents a pail.

You can learn about SAD . . .

and GLAD . . .

and MAD!

There are
so many things
you can learn about.
BUT . . . you'll miss
the best things
if you keep
your eyes shut.

The more that you read,
the more things you will know.
The more that you learn,
the more places you'll go.

You might learn
a way to earn
a few dollars.

Or how to make doughnuts . . .

or kangaroo collars.

You can learn to read music
and play a Hut-Zut
if you keep your eyes open.
But <u>not</u> with them shut.

If you read with your eyes shut
you're likely to find
that the place where you're going
is far, far behind.

WELCOME to WILKES-BARRE
DALLAS
SAN DIEGO
LAKE FOREST
SCHENECTADY
DETOUR
Bikes Only
NO EXIT
NO RIGHT TURN
LEFT
?
STOP
REST ROOMS 128 Miles
SALINA Kansas Birthplace of Curtis A. Abel 2376 Miles →
XYZ
ABC

SO...
that's why I tell you
to keep your eyes wide.
Keep them wide open...
at least on one side.

Learning to read is fun with Beginner Books

I CAN READ IT ALL BY MYSELF

Beginner Books

FIRST get started with:

Ten Apples Up On Top
Dr. Seuss

Go Dog Go
P D Eastman

Put Me in the Zoo
Robert LopShire

THEN gain confidence with:

Dr. Seuss's ABC*
Dr. Seuss

Fox in Sox*
Dr. Seuss

Green Eggs and Ham*
Dr. Seuss

Hop on Pop*
Dr. Seuss

I Can Read With My Eyes Shut
Dr. Seuss

I Wish That I Had Duck Feet
Dr. Seuss

One Fish, Two Fish*
Dr. Seuss

Oh, the Thinks You Can Think!
Dr. Seuss

Please Try to Remember the First of October
Dr. Seuss

Wacky Wednesday
Dr. Seuss

Are You My Mother?
P D Eastman

Because a Little Bug Went Ka-choo!
Rosetta Stone

Best Nest
P D Eastman

Come Over to My House
Theo. LeSieg

The Digging-est Dog
Al Perkins

I Am Not Going to Get Up Today!
Theo. LeSieg

It's Not Easy Being a Bunny!
Marilyn Sadler

I Want to Be Somebody New
Robert LopShire

Maybe You Should Fly a Jet!
Theo. LeSieg

Robert the Rose Horse
Joan Heilbroner

The Very Bad Bunny
Joan Heilbroner

THEN take off with:

The Cat in the Hat*
Dr. Seuss

The Cat in the Hat Comes Back*
Dr. Seuss

Oh Say Can You Say?
Dr. Seuss

My Book About Me
Dr. Seuss

A Big Ball of String
Marion Holland

Chitty Chitty Bang Bang!
Ian Fleming

A Fish Out of Water
Helen Palmer

A Fly Went By
Mike McClintock

The King, the Mice and the Cheese
N & E Gurney

Sam and the Firefly
P D Eastman

BERENSTAIN BEAR BOOKS
By Stan & Jan Berenstain

The Bear Detectives

The Bear Scouts

The Bears' Christmas

The Bears' Holiday

The Bears' Picnic

The Berenstain Bears and the Missing Dinosaur Bones

The Big Honey Hunt

The Bike Lesson

THEN you won't quite be ready to go to college. But you'll be well on your way!

*From the Dr. Seuss Classic Collection